Bravo to all my family members and friends who pursue careers in the arts—
H.Z.

To Kinga—
J.D.

Text copyright © 2013 Harriet Ziefert
Illustrations copyright © 2013 by Jenni Desmond
All rights reserved/CIP data is available.
Published in the United States 2013 by
🍎 Blue Apple Books, 515 Valley Street,
Maplewood, NJ 07040
www.blueapplebooks.com
First Edition
Printed in China 03/13
ISBN: 978-1-60905-286-7
1 3 5 7 9 10 8 6 4 2

I am a backstage cat.
My owner is a celebrity.
I ride with her to the theater
in a big, silver-grey limousine.

We go inside through the stage door. It's early—
way before show time. There are no fans waiting.

We go straight to the dressing room.

I prefer to walk by myself, but my leading lady
is in a hurry and carries me the whole way.

I watch as
my leading lady
gets ready.

She needs:

rouge and powder . . .

eyelashes . . .

lipstick . . .

bracelets . . .

a wig . . .

shoes . . .

and her costume!

We hear the announcement,
"Five minutes to curtain!"

Then my lady says,
"Bye, Simon. Be good!
I'll be back at intermission."

But before
the door closes . . .

I spy something interesting in the hall.
I run through the open door.

Where am I? There is so much to see—
furniture, lights, props, and costumes.

Onstage, I see
two people talking.
I don't think they
notice me.

Then, before I have time to figure out what's going on . . .

I hear a loud

THUMP!

Something big just dropped!

I freeze!

Then
I run!

I go straight . . .

straight onto
the stage!

Lucky me, I see some
white birch trees.
I run to the nearest one
and start to climb.

When I reach the top, I curl up
and try to make myself invisible.

Then I hear a loud voice:

"Simon, I am
the stage manager.
Come down!
The show must go on!"

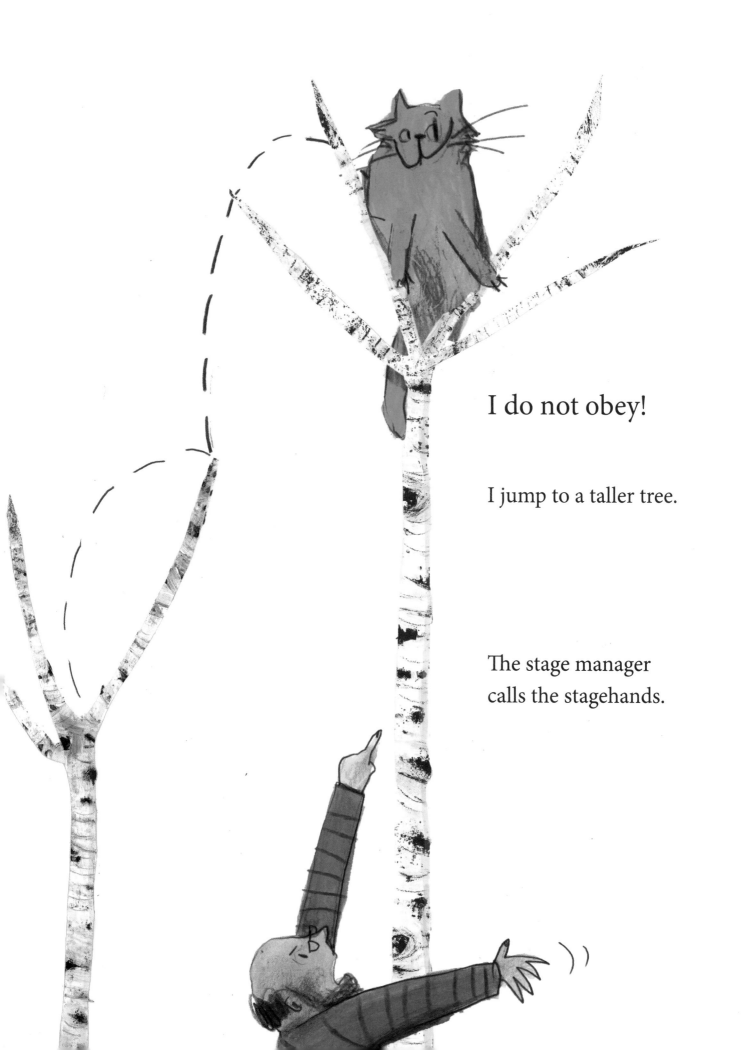

I do not obey!

I jump to a taller tree.

The stage manager
calls the stagehands.

One of them shouts:

"Simon, I am
a stagehand.
I have food
for you.

Come down!
The show must
go on!"

I do not want a tuna fish sandwich.

I take a flying leap onto a chandelier.

The stagehand
calls the electricians.

One of them screams:

"Simon, I am in charge
of the lighting.

You cannot swing
from the chandelier!

Just jump down!
I will catch you."

I climb higher
and perch between
two spotlights.

I don't want to jump
into the arms of
the electrician!

I hear yelling from
the stagehands:

"Simon, we can see you.
You cannot hide from us!"

"We are getting nowhere," says the stage manager.

"Call the leading lady. It's her cat.
Maybe she can get him to come down."

My leading lady
speaks softly.

"Simon, please,
please come down.
I will hold you
and kiss your head,
just the way you like it.
Then you can
watch the show."

She sings to me:

When you're feeling all alone,
   I'll be here.
If you're out all on your own,
   I'll be here.

      No matter how far you wander,
         No matter how far you roam,
      Just remember
         I will always be around
         When you want to come back home.

It's fun to travel far and wide,
   But sometimes it's so lonely,
Unless there's someone
   By your side.

      So when you feel sad and blue,
         I'll be here.
      Don't forget I'll come through.
      I'll be here.
         I'll be here.

I relax.

I want to be close to
the beautiful sounds,
so I climb down carefully.

My leading lady keeps
her promise.
She kisses my face.

She gives me a special seat
in the wings.

And she says,
"Do not move from this chair.
I expect to find you here
at the end of the show!"

The orchestra tunes up,
cast members take their positions,
and the show goes on!

But during the third scene . . .

an unwanted character
runs across the stage.

I can be a star, too!

After the show, we both sign autographs
at the stage door!